CYCLOPS

of CENTRAL PARK

MADELYN ROSENBERG

illustrated by **VICTORIA TENTLER-KRYLOV**

putnam

G. P. Putnam's Sons

For my flock: You help me be brave —M.R.

For my boys, big and small, who lived and laughed through this book with me —V. T.-K.

G. P. PUTNAM'S SONS
An imprint of Penguin Random House LLC, New York

Text copyright © 2020 by Madelyn Rosenberg. Illustrations copyright © 2020 by Victoria Tentler-Krylov.
Penguin supports copyright. Copyright fuels creativity, encourages diverse voices, promotes free speech, and creates a vibrant culture. Thank you for buying an authorized edition of this book and for complying with copyright laws by not reproducing, scanning, or distributing any part of it in any form without permission. You are supporting writers and allowing Penguin to continue to publish books for every reader.

G. P. Putnam's Sons is a registered trademark of Penguin Random House LLC.

Visit us online at penguinrandomhouse.com

Library of Congress Cataloging-in-Publication Data
Names: Rosenberg, Madelyn, 1966– author. | Tentler-Krylov, Victoria, illustrator. | Title: Cyclops of Central Park / Madelyn Rosenberg; illustrated by Victoria Tentler-Krylov. Description: New York: G. P. Putnam's Sons, [2020] | Summary: Timid Cyclops ventures out of his cave in Central Park to seek Eugene, a daring sheep missing from his flock, all across New York City. | Identifiers: LCCN 2019017696 (print) | LCCN 2019020627 (ebook) | ISBN 9780525514732 (ebook) | ISBN 9780525514718 (ebook) | ISBN 9780525514701 (hardcover) | Subjects: | CYAC: Adventure and adventurers—Fiction. | Cyclopes (Greek mythology)—Fiction. | Sheep—Fiction. | Central Park (New York, N.Y.)—Fiction. | New York (N.Y.)—Fiction. Classification: LCC PZ7.R71897 (ebook) | LCC PZ7.R71897 Cyc 2020 (print) | DDC [E]—dc23 | LC record available at https://lccn.loc.gov/2019017696

Manufactured in China by RR Donnelley Asia Printing Solutions Ltd.
ISBN 9780525514701
10 9 8 7 6 5 4 3 2 1

Design by Eileen Savage. Text set in Clasica Slab.
The art for this book was painted in watercolor and gouache, and completed with Adobe Photoshop.

Late at night, just before he closed his eye and went to sleep in his Central Park cave, Cyclops counted his sheep.

When the sun rose, he counted them again, and that's when he noticed—"... sixteen, seventeen..." —one of them was missing.

He knew who it was, of course.

"Eugene?"

It was always Eugene.

Cyclops looked behind the ficus tree and under the bed.

He searched the meadow where the sheep often stood, taking in the view. The meadow was empty.

Cyclops bit his nails. He had explained 1,022 times about the dangers that lurked nearby. The grass was too sharp. The carousel was too twirly. The new restaurant on Fifth Avenue did not serve spaghetti.

"There's no place like cave,"
Cyclops had told Eugene.

"There's no place like world,"
Eugene had told Cyclops.

Now Eugene was out in the world. Cyclops had to find him. And he had to make sure the rest of the sheep stayed safe.

"Stay near cave," he warned his flock. "Beware of grass. Beware of everything." He hugged each sheep. Then he went off to find Eugene.

He searched high above the city . . .

and hit all of the major hot spots. He thought he spied the missing sheep in SoHo—and again at the Guggenheim. But his eye was playing tricks on him.

"Eugene?"

"No. It's a de Kooning."

When Cyclops stepped too close to the art, the security guards suggested he try viewing it from farther away. They escorted him out of the museum, where he was trampled by wild tourists and conked on the head with a salami.

Next, Cyclops made posters and stapled copies everywhere. But with all of the lights and billboards, they were often overlooked.

LOST SHEEP

HAIR: CURLY EYES: BROWN
enjoys: sunsets, hay, martial arts films
last seen: Central Park
answers to: Eugene

He searched in the
Yankees' dugout. But he
struck out there, too.

Eugene had often urged Cyclops to take the flock to the Statue of Liberty.

"Too green," Cyclops had said.

This time, he mustered his courage—and his life jacket—and boarded a ferry. He kept a sharp eye out for sharks the whole way there. But Cyclops did not find any sharks in the New York City harbor.

And he did not
find Eugene.

The city was every bit as terrifying as Cyclops had suspected. He needed reinforcements.

The sheep lined up, ready for their mission. They had magnifying glasses. They had walkie-talkies. And they had a pretty good idea of where Eugene had gone.

The subway was crowded, but the other passengers politely gave up their seats. Cyclops and his flock had a car all to themselves.

They held on tight and disembarked
at the appropriate station.

"Eugene?"

"Eugene?"   "Eugene!"

There he was, atop the Cyclone, his hooves waving in the air.

"Too high!" Cyclops shouted. "Too scary. Too wobbly. Too FAST!"

"Just riiiiiiiiiiiiiiiiiiight!" yelled Eugene.

When the ride was over, Eugene held out a long roll of tickets.

Cyclops's hand was too shaky to take one.

"There's no place like cave," he said.

"There's no place like world," Eugene told him.

"Pretty please?" said the flock.

Cyclops took a deep breath and closed his eye. He tried his favorite yoga pose.

He thought for a very long time. Then he took a giant gulp and got in line with his flock.

Together, Cyclops and all eighteen sheep rode the Cyclone.

At first, Cyclops couldn't look.
Then he peeked between his fingers
and saw . . . the whole world.

When the ride was over, he got in line again.

Cyclops and the sheep
rode the Wonder Wheel and
the bumper cars.

When they went wading in the foamy deep, the only shark they saw was the one around Cyclops's waist. Next, Cyclops ate a record number of hot dogs and treated the sheep to some cotton candy.

Finally, it was time to return home.

As they crossed the Gapstow Bridge, they stopped to watch the sun set over Manhattan. The city was not as terrifying as Cyclops had thought—as long as he was with his flock.

"There's no place like world," Cyclops said.

"There's no place like cave," yawned Eugene.

And they were both exactly right.

That night, just before he went to sleep,
Cyclops counted his sheep.
    "Sixteen, seventeen . . . eighteen!"

Then he sat outside his cozy cave—

" . . . thirty-five, thirty-six . . ."
—and counted all of the things they
were going to do next.